BIG BUCKS

THE FAST CASH OF STOCK CAR RACING

JOANNE MATTERN

Children's Press®
A Division of Scholastic Inc.
New York / Toronto / London / Auckland / Sydney
Mexico City / New Delhi / Hong Kong
Danbury, Connecticut

Book Design: Michelle Innes
Contributing Editor: Geeta Sobha

Photo Credits: Cover © Todd Warshaw/Getty Images for NASCAR; pg. 4 © Victor Blackman/Express/Getty Images; pg. 6 © Chris Stanford/Getty Images; pgs. 7, 11 © Darrell Ingham/Getty Images; pg. 13 © Jon Ferrey/Allsport; pg. 14 © Jamie Squire/Getty Images; pgs. 16, 31 © Robert Laberge/Getty Images; pgs. 20, 34 © Nick Laham/Getty Images; pg. 21 © Doug Pensinger/Getty Images; pgs. 23, 27 © Jonathan Ferrey/Getty Images; pg. 24 © Chris Graythen/Getty Images; pg. 33 © Ronald Martinez/Getty Images; pg. 36 STR/AFP/Getty Images; pg. 41 © Rusty Jarrett/Getty Images

Library of Congress Cataloging-in-Publication Data

Mattern, Joanne, 1963–
    Big bucks : the fast cash of stock car racing / Joanne Mattern.
    p. cm.—(Stock car racing)
    Includes index
    ISBN-10: 0-531-16807-7 (lib. bdg.)   0-531-18715-2 (pbk.)
    ISBN-13: 978-0-531-16807-3 (lib. bdg.) 978-0-531-18715-9 (pbk.)
    1. Stock car racing—United States—Pictorial works—Juvenile literature.
    2. NASCAR (Association)—Juvenile literature. 3. Stock car drivers—United States—Pictorial works—Juvenile literature. I. Title. II. Series: Stock car racing (Children's Press)

GV1029.9.S74M328 2007
796.72-dc22
                                                        2006010975

TABLE OF CONTENTS

Early NASCAR race cars were regular cars that were not built strong enough for racing. Today's stock cars are specially built racing machines.

The cheers of forty-five hundred fans fill your ears. These people have all paid fifty cents per ticket to see this NASCAR race. Your heart is pounding as you rev the engine of your car, which you have modified for high-speed racing. Driving the last lap, you whiz by the other racers. Then your heart sinks as cars on the left and right pass you. Who will win this race? You push your car to its limits in hopes of winning a prize! The prize that awaits the lap leaders is a bottle of rum. There are also a case of motor oil, a case of beer, a box of cigars, a $2.50 credit at a clothing store, and a $25 credit toward a car from a used-car lot.

Surprised at the ticket price and the prizes described here? Well, this race harks back about seventy years to July 4, 1938, to the first NASCAR race in Daytona Beach, Florida. NASCAR stands for the National Association of Stock Car Auto Racing. Bill France spent months organizing this race and finding drivers to participate in it. At the end of the race, Bill France and his partner, Charlie Reese, paid their bills. Then they split the profits from the race. France and Reese each walked away with two hundred dollars.

Stock car races have changed a great deal over the decades. Today, NASCAR races are held before huge crowds. Drivers race million-dollar cars at modern speedways. Instead of motor oil or clothing, they

In February 2006, about 200,000 people attended the Daytona 500, one of the largest NASCAR events. The average ticket price for a race is $85.

receive tens of thousands of dollars in prize money. The NASCAR organization itself makes a lot more than two hundred dollars on a race!

So much of the sports world today has to do with making money and spending money. NASCAR is no different. Let's take a look at how much it costs to race in NASCAR and how much money can be made in this fast-moving sport.

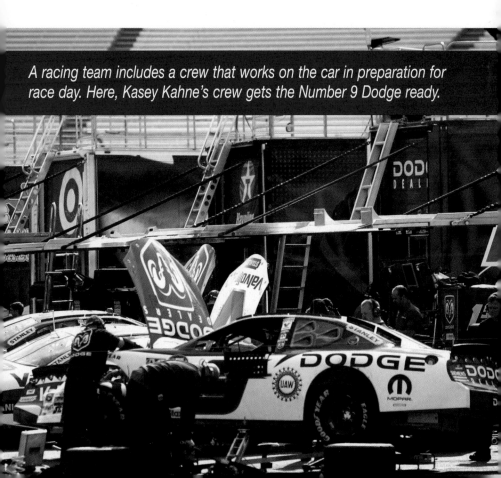

A racing team includes a crew that works on the car in preparation for race day. Here, Kasey Kahne's crew gets the Number 9 Dodge ready.

CHAPTER ONE

PRIZES AND SALARIES

The world of NASCAR is very different today than it was in 1938. NASCAR has become a big business, generating an enormous amount of profit. Some of the largest corporations in the United States sponsor racing teams. Car manufacturers put millions of dollars into creating the best and fastest cars. NASCAR drivers earn money in many different ways. For example, when they win races, they collect their share of prize money. Also, both drivers and cars display the logos of their sponsors in return for money. In fact, the sport could not exist without sponsors and the big money they provide.

TOP DOLLARS FOR TOP DRIVERS

The Nextel Cup is the highest level of racing in NASCAR. Drivers who are just starting out in Nextel Cup racing can earn a salary of about $100,000 a year. Their salaries are paid by the owners of the cars they drive. Drivers with more Nextel Cup experience can earn between $100,000 and $200,000. The top drivers earn between $500,000 and $800,000 a year.

The driver's salary is not the only way he or she earns money. Drivers also get a percentage of the purse, or prize money. New drivers earn about 10 percent of the prize. The top drivers can get up to 50 percent of the prize money. When Dale Earnhardt, Jr., won the Daytona 500 in 2004, he took home about $1.5 million.

Prize money comes from several different sources. The company that owns the track where the race is held puts up the most money. The larger the racetrack, the bigger the purse. That is because larger racetracks can hold more people. So a big track will make more money than a small track because it will sell more tickets.

TELEVISION PAYS

Another source of prize money comes from television. Today, NASCAR races are broadcast by three networks: the FOX Broadcasting Company (FOX), the National Broadcasting Company (NBC), and the Turner Network Television (TNT). Each network pays money to NASCAR to air the races. NASCAR puts part of that money into prizes for the drivers. About 25 percent of television earnings, or revenue, goes into the purse.

The prize money put up by the television networks is paid on a decreasing scale. The first-place driver

WHERE DOES THE TV MONEY GO?

Average TV contract: $400 million per season
Number of races per season: 36
Average payment per race: $11.1 million
65% to track owner: $7.2 million
25% to prize money: $2.7 million
10% to NASCAR: $1.1 million

Highly skilled mechanics and engineers draw top-dollar salaries for their specialized work.

wins the most money. The second-place driver wins the second-highest amount, and so on.

BONUS BUCKS

Through bonus payments, a NASCAR team can make a lot of money even if its driver does not win. The practice of bonus payments goes back to NASCAR's beginnings. In the early days of stock car racing, most races were held in the southeastern part of the United States. NASCAR, however, sponsored races in Arizona, California, and other western states. Team owners were not sure if they wanted to spend the time and money to travel so far. So NASCAR guaranteed the top teams that they would make extra money just for showing up. The plan worked, and NASCAR was able to have a full lineup of cars for races in the West.

Today, money from bonus payments can lead to some odd results. For example, in July 2002, Jimmie Johnson finished fourth in the Winston Cup, now called the Nextel Cup. He earned more than $88,000. In the same year, Jeff Burton finished in thirty-ninth place. However, Burton took home almost $98,000! He got that amount because his team received a bonus payout.

Back in November 1999, Dale Jarrett won the Pennzoil 400. He also won the prize of $2,000,000!

Some drivers are unhappy with bonus payments to teams that do not win. Most drivers and teams, though, agree that the system works. Driver Kyle Petty says, "I'm not going to say that the system is perfect, but the system rewards the teams that perform and win races and rewards the teams that run all of the races." NASCAR's managing director of business operations, Kevin Triplett, agrees: "Every major sport rewards consistent performers. It's the same concept, it's just done differently."

Kyle Petty, son of racing great Richard Petty, won his first race in 1979.

NASCAR has its own bonus program called the Winner's Circle. This bonus payment goes to the top ten winners from the previous season, plus the first two winners in the current season. This bonus ensures that NASCAR's top drivers go to every race. NASCAR also pays a bonus to any team in a race that is in the top thirty in points.

FAST FACT

Jeff Gordon holds the Guinness World Record for the highest career earnings in NASCAR. From 1992 to 2005, Gordon earned $73,587,373!

GAINING POINTS

Points are another way drivers and car owners can increase the amount of money they get. Starting in 1975, drivers and owners were given points after every race. The number of points depended on where the driver finishes in the race. The winner of the race receives 175 points. Second place is worth 170 points. The points get smaller until they reach last place. That driver receives only thirty-four points.

Jeff Green won the Bud Pole Award, which pays $5000, at the Daytona 500 in 2003.

In addition, a driver can score bonus points. Any driver who leads a lap gets five extra points. The driver who leads the most laps also gets five extra points. These points determine a team's standing— and therefore, how much money the drivers and owners will earn.

GATORADE FRONT RUNNER AWARD

The driver who leads the most laps in a race can win the Gatorade Front Runner Award, which is sponsored by the Quaker Oats Company. This award pays a $10,000 bonus to the race leader at the halfway mark of a race. After the seventeenth race of the season, there is a $30,000 bonus for the driver with the most Gatorade Front Runner points. At the end of the racing season, the driver with the most Front Runner points wins $50,000.

CHAPTER TWO

THE ALL-IMPORTANT SPONSOR

Stock car racing is a very expensive sport. Owners must come up with enough money to pay for the car, the driver, and many other expenses. So where does the money come from? The answer is corporate sponsors. Without corporate sponsors, NASCAR teams would not be able to afford to race.

Sponsors invest heavily in NASCAR. A company will

spend at least five million dollars to sponsor a Nextel Cup team for a season. The more successful a team is, the more sponsorship money it will get. A top team can bring in more than ten million dollars in sponsorships. This is a lot of money, but the teams need it. That money pays for a team's car and other equipment. It pays the salaries of the drivers, mechanics, and other members of the team. Teams use sponsorship funds for traveling to and from race sites and many other expenses.

WHAT'S IN A NAME?

Sponsors pay for their names to be part of NASCAR. This happens in many ways. Just look at the names of the races and you will see how important corporate sponsors are to NASCAR. NASCAR races are usually named after sponsors. For example, the DieHard 500 is sponsored by DieHard, the maker of automotive batteries. Guess who sponsors the Pepsi 400 or the Coca-Cola 600?!

Sponsorship goes far beyond the names of the races. Cars are covered with logos with the names of many different companies. Drivers wear their sponsors' names and symbols on their uniforms.

Sponsors pay a lot of money to have their logo or name associated with a driver and his vehicle.

Drivers help their sponsors by making personal appearances. This is another way for the sponsor to get attention. Drivers go to events to sign autographs and talk to fans in order to promote their sponsors' products.

Tony Stewart won the Pepsi 400 at Daytona International Speedway in 2005. This race, is of course, sponsored by the Pepsi-Cola Company.

TYPES OF SPONSORS

There are several levels of sponsorship. Primary sponsors spend the most money. This type of sponsorship can cost between ten million and fifteen million dollars. In return for the money, the racing team shows the sponsor's name and logo on the hood of the driver's car. This is the best place to advertise

Tony Stewart's primary sponsor, Home Depot, definitely gets prime placement on his Number 20 Chevrolet Monte Carlo SS.

because it is so easy to see. Primary sponsors also get the most visible locations on uniforms.

Some companies cannot afford to be primary sponsors. These companies pay less and become associate sponsors. An associate sponsor does not get prime advertising space on the team's cars and uniforms. The driver will not do as many personal appearances for that company. The company, however,

THE RISING COST OF SPONSORSHIP

Fred Lorenzen was one of the first drivers to take on a sponsor. During the late 1960s, he got a Ford car dealership in Fayetteville, North Carolina, to pay him six thousand dollars for every twenty-nine-race season. That worked out to about two hundred dollars for each race. By the late 1980s, costs had risen tremendously. Racer Junior Johnson said that he needed about three million dollars in sponsorships in a thirty-race season to break even. That is about $100,000 a race. By the year 2000, the sponsorship costs had risen even higher. During that season, United Parcel Service (UPS) sponsored Dale Jarrett for about $15 million per year. That's about $400,000 per race!

Reed Sorenson (left) and Jamie McMurray (right) are covered in sponsors' logos. They know that without sponsorship money, they cannot afford to be a part of NASCAR.

still gets exposure and a way to advertise itself. The company logo may go on a less visible area. An associate sponsorship can cost between two million and six million dollars.

Dozens of major corporations are represented at NASCAR racing events.

SPONSOR PRIZES

Each race has contingency sponsors. These sponsors pay prizes to winning drivers who display the sponsors' logos on their cars. So if a winning car has the logo of Sunoco Gasoline on his or her car, that driver will win a contingency prize from Sunoco.

Contingency funds have been around since the earliest days of NASCAR. They used to be called "tow money." The purpose of this type of prize money was to make sure teams had enough funds to make it to the next race. Without this money, some teams might not have been able to race very often.

Contingency money is for such achievements as leading during the most laps. To win these prizes, the driver has to display the sponsor's logo or name on his or her car. For example, a driver could get five thousand dollars for winning the MCI Fast Pace Award if he or she runs the fastest lap. However, the prize will only be awarded if the driver has an MCI sticker on his car. No sticker—no prize! This type of sponsorship allows companies to advertise on a number of cars without giving a large amount of money to just one team.

TOO CORPORATE

Many fans dislike corporate sponsorships. They say that sponsorships make races too commercial. Sponsorships can also put a lot of pressure on a driver. A new driver usually cannot choose who sponsors him or her. The driver has to take any sponsor who offers to pay the bills. This can be a problem if the driver does not like that sponsor's products. Is it fair to the driver to advertise a product he or she does not believe in? Is it right for that driver to say good things about a product he or she does not want to use? Most people would say no.

Sponsors argue that they provide a valuable service to NASCAR teams. Without money from the sponsors, most—if not all—teams would be unable to race! The cost of NASCAR is simply too high. Like it or not, corporate sponsorship is here to stay.

A NASCAR race is a sea of different colors. Each car's colors are determined by the sponsoring company and its brand logos.

CHAPTER THREE

TRACKS PAVED WITH GOLD

Racetracks are not owned and operated by NASCAR. Instead, most of them are owned by big corporations. Most of the racetracks that host Nextel Cup events are owned by two companies. The largest company is International Speedway Corporation. It was started by Bill France, the same person who started NASCAR.

Today, the France family still runs International Speedway Corporation.

The second biggest company is Speedway Motorsports. Speedway Motorsports and International Speedway Corporation own more than two-thirds of the tracks used for Nextel Cup racing. The other tracks are owned by small companies or families.

Racetrack owners have a major financial stake in hosting NASCAR events. They pay a lot of money to host NASCAR races. They are also responsible for advertising and promoting the NASCAR event. After all, there is a great amount of money to be made by racetrack owners each year.

HOSTING NASCAR

Track owners must first pay NASCAR a fee to host a race. In return, NASCAR manages the race. These fees can range from $150,000 for a small race to $500,000 for a large race.

Track owners must also pay the prize money. They also pay all the operating costs of holding a race. These costs include salaries, security, first aid, and food for the spectators. Most tracks hire one person for every seventy-five fans at an event. That means there can be between one thousand and two thousand employees working various jobs at the track on a race day.

PAYBACK

Of course, racetrack owners do not just spend money on races. They make money, too! Track owners earn money, or revenue, in several different ways. Most of their money comes from ticket sales. The price depends on the race and the seat. A ticket can cost as little as thirty-five dollars or almost as much as two hundred dollars.

Every track has luxury suites. These are enclosed, air-conditioned rooms from which fans can view races. Food and drinks are served there. Luxury suites are usually rented by corporations. A one-year lease at the Daytona International Speedway can cost between $40,000 and $130,000.

Track owners also make a profit from the parking lots. Fans can even camp on the infield for a fee, as some NASCAR events take place over the course of a few days. The infield is the area that the track surrounds. All together, a track owner earns about 70 percent of his or her revenue from ticket sales, suite rentals, parking, and camping fees.

The Dover International Speedway was originally a track meant for both car races and horse races.

Food, souvenirs, programs, and advertising also add to the track owners' profits. Advertisers pay the track owner to put up ads around the track. The television network that broadcasts the race also pays a fee to the track owner.

A racetrack owner can earn a lot of money. A Nextel Cup race at a large track can bring in as much as ten million dollars in revenue. The track owner will pay between five and six million dollars to host the race. That leaves the owner with a profit of about 40 percent, or about four million dollars.

FANS EXPECT THE BEST

In the past, racetracks were cheap to build and run. Fans did not expect comfortable seats. They did not expect a lot of food. They just wanted to sit down and watch the race. Today, fans are used to going to sports stadiums. They are used to modern bathrooms, a variety of food stands, and comfortable seats. In order to compete with stadiums, NASCAR tracks must offer more services. This raises the cost of running a racetrack even more.

Parking garages are an important feature at modern race tracks. Today's race tracks have multiple garages to house all the cars.

LAYING DOWN TRACKS

Building a racetrack is very expensive. The biggest expense is buying land. Fifty years ago, land was cheap. Today, owners can expect to pay millions of dollars to buy enough land to build a track.

Owners must also get permission from the local government. They explain that a NASCAR track can

The Martinsville Speedway in Virginia is the shortest track to host Nextel Cup races. It is only .526 miles (.846 km) long.

bring a tremendous amount of
money into a community.
Rick Horrow worked
with International
Speedway
Corporation to
locate new places
to build tracks.
He would tell
local officials,
"Race fans travel
three hundred miles
on average to come to a
race, they stay for two to three
days, and spend approximately two hundred and
eighty dollars per day." This can add up to about
seventy million dollars in revenue for local businesses,
such as hotels and restaurants, for one big NASCAR
event. Track owners also pay taxes on their property.
This makes even more money for local governments.

FAST FACT

The Daytona 500 is probably the most famous NASCAR race. The Daytona International Speedway is owned by International Speedway Corporation.

TAX DOLLARS

In return for the revenue earned by local government,
the track owner expects financial help from that

Stock car racing is spreading throughout the world. In this photo, a track is being built in Shanghai, China.

government. Racetracks, like sports stadiums, are usually built using public money. For example, in 2005, International Speedway Corporation needed about $332 million to build a speedway in Washington's Kitsap County. The company asked the Washington state legislature to pass a bill to pay $166 million toward this project. Some of the funds would be raised through taxes. The government would also borrow some of the money.

International Speedway offered to pay the other $166 million. The company argued that Washington State would make back its money quickly through revenue brought into the local economy. In the end, the government was not convinced. Early in 2006, the bill was withdrawn.

Just like everything else in NASCAR, racetracks are expensive to build and run. The costs of other parts of the sport keep going up, too.

CHAPTER FOUR

THE RISING COST OF RACING

In 1969, Richard Childress started racing in NASCAR. Childress built and raced his own car. "I built it for four hundred dollars and had a racing budget of one thousand dollars," he said. Today, NASCAR teams need between $750,000 and one million a year. Owners do not build their own cars anymore. Today, NASCAR race cars are built by major corporations, such as Ford or Dodge. These companies spend at least $125 million per year on NASCAR cars. They are constantly testing new designs and building new cars.

Automobile companies provide parts for the cars to run. The stock car's engine alone can cost more than $70,000. A single tire can cost $400. A team uses a dozen or more sets of four tires during every race. That means a team's tire bill per race can add up to about $20,000! The top racing teams have a budget of at least $150,000 per race. That figure does not even include the cost of paying the teams' salaries.

RACING BILLS

Although there is a lot of money to be won in NASCAR events, there are times when teams cannot afford to race. In the past few years, people have worried about the rising costs of racing in NASCAR. Drivers who do not have sponsors have been forced to stop racing. Owners who used to run several cars every season have cut back to just one or two cars. Joe Gibbs, the owner of Joe Gibbs Racing, said, "You can't race in this series and try and win it without losing money."

NASCAR is worried about rising costs, too. In February 2004, it had trouble finding forty-three cars to fill a couple of Nextel Cup races. Brian France, the chief executive officer (CEO) of NASCAR, has made cutting costs one of his most important goals. NASCAR is working with car companies to design simpler engines. These engines will not be as expensive to buy or to run. NASCAR also may limit the number of tests a new car goes through. NASCAR made this decision because many owners complained about the high costs of testing.

MOVING AHEAD

Despite the expensive cost of racing, NASCAR is still a successful and powerful business. Sponsors and television networks pour money into NASCAR because it is such a popular sport. Fans spend money on tickets,

FAST FACT

Brian France is the grandson of Bill France. Bill France started NASCAR. So NASCAR is still a family-run business!

souvenirs, and NASCAR products. Teams spend money to run the best cars and hire the best drivers.

Many businesses involved in NASCAR are publicly owned companies. For example, stocks for the Speedway Motorsports Inc. are traded on the New York Stock Exchange. NASCAR drivers race on tracks made of dirt or pavement, but there is gold on those NASCAR tracks!

NASCAR drivers make an appearance at the New York Stock Exchange to kick off a day of trading.

NEW WORDS

bonus (**boh**-nuhss) an extra reward given for doing something well

budget (**buhj**-it) a plan for how money will be earned and spent

contingency (kuhn-**tin**-juhn-see) something that will happen as a result of something else

commercial (kuh-**mur**-shuhl) to do with buying and selling things

lap (**lap**) one time around something, such as a racetrack

legislature (**lej**-iss-lay-chur) a group of people who have the power to make or change laws for a country or state

logo (**loh**-goh) a symbol that represents a company or organization

NEW WORDS

mechanic (muh-kan-ik) someone who is skilled at operating or repairing machinery

profit (prof-it) the amount of money left after the costs of running a business have been subtracted from the money earned

revenue (rev-uh-noo) money that is made from investments

salary (sal-uh-ree) the fixed amount of money someone is paid for his or her work

sponsor (spon-sur) a person or company that pays money in return for advertisement

suite (sweet) a group of rooms that are connected

FOR FURTHER READING

Buckley, James, Jr. *Eyewitness NASCAR*. New York: DK
    Publishing, Inc., 2005.

The Official NASCAR Handbook. New York: HarperCollins
    Publishers, 1998.

Owens, Thomas S., and Diana Star Helmer. *NASCAR*.
    Brookfield, CT: Twenty-First Century Books, 2000.

RESOURCES

ORGANIZATION

NASCAR
PO Box 2875
Daytona Beach, FL 32120
http://www.nascar.com/

RESOURCES

WEB SITES

Fast Machines

www.fastmachines.com

Get all the latest information on NASCAR racing at this Web site.

How NASCAR Splits the Money

nascar.about.com/cs/nascar101/a/payouts.htm

The article presented at this site gives details about how NASCAR cash is awarded.

Motorsports Hall of Fame of America

www.mshf.com

This site has information on all types of racing, including stock car racing. Click on the stock cars link to read all about stock car racers who have made history.

INDEX

INDEX

ABOUT THE AUTHOR

Joanne Mattern has written more than two hundred books for children. Her favorite topics include sports, history, animals, and biographies. Joanne lives in New York State with her husband, three daughters, and three cats.

DATE DUE

JAN 0 3			
JAN 1 0			
APR 1 9			
MAY 1 0			
FEB 1 2			
APR 2 1			
DEC 0 7 2011			
DEC 1 3 2012			
OCT 0 4 2013			
MAR 3			
OCT 0 6 2014			
NOV 1 0 2014			
NOV 2 7 2014			